降去神通

AVATAR
THE LAST AIRBENDER.

AANG'S
School Days

adapted by Michael Teitelbaum
based on the teleplay *The Headband* by John O'Bryan
illustrated by Patrick Spaziante

Ready-to-Read

Simon Spotlight
New York   London   Toronto   Sydney

Based on the TV series *Nickelodeon Avatar: The Last Airbender*™
as seen on Nickelodeon®

SIMON SPOTLIGHT
An imprint of Simon & Schuster Children's Publishing Division
1230 Avenue of the Americas, New York, New York 10020
Manufactured in the United States of America
First Edition
2 4 6 8 10 9 7 5 3 1
Library of Congress Cataloging-in-Publication Data
Teitelbaum, Michael.
Aang's school days / adapted by Michael Teitelbaum ; based on the teleplay The headband,
by John O'Bryan ; illustrated by Patrick Spaziante. – 1st ed.
p. cm. — (Ready-to-read)
"Based on the TV series Nickelodeon Avatar: the last airbender, as seen on Nickelodeon"—
T.p. verso.
I. Spaziante, Patrick. II. Avatar, the last airbender (Television program) III. Title.
PZ7.T233Aa 2008 [E]–dc22 2007028176
ISBN-13: 978-1-4169-5813-0
ISBN-10: 1-4169-5813-4

CHAPTER ONE

My name is Aang. I am the Avatar.

My friends, Sokka, Katara, Toph, and I are in the Fire Nation trying to learn all we can about them.

Momo, my pet flying lemur, is with us too. We're all traveling on Appa, my flying bison and my best buddy.

Appa landed and we found a cave to hide in.

"We need some Fire Nation clothes so we can blend in," Katara said. "Then we won't have to hide in a cave all the time."

We found clothes hanging on a clothesline.

"I don't know about this," I said. "These belong to somebody."

"I call the silk robe!" Katara shouted, before snatching the robe.

"I guess it's okay if we just borrow them," I said. "I call the suit!"

We all got dressed in our Fire Nation outfits. Then I put on a headband to hide my Avatar tattoo. "Ta-da! Now I look like a normal Fire Nation kid."

Now that we were dressed like Fire Nation folk, we could go wherever we wanted. We headed to a bazaar in the center of a village. Momo hid inside my jacket.

"I used to visit my friend Kuzon here a hundred years ago," I explained. "So I know their customs. Watch me."

"Greetings, my good hotman," I said to a stranger. That's how we greeted one another back when I visited Kuzon.

My friends went into a restaurant that only served meat. I don't eat meat, so I waited outside.

Suddenly three Fire Nation soldiers came up to me. "It's over. We caught you," one of them said.

"Who, me?" I asked nervously.

"It is obvious you don't belong here," the soldier said firmly.

Uh, oh! I am in trouble. They must know I am the Avatar!

CHAPTER TWO

I was ready for a fight, but the soldier said, "Next time you play hooky, you might want to take off your school uniform."

Whew! They think I'm playing hooky!

I thought I could learn something from a Fire Nation school, so I didn't say anything when the soldiers took me there.

All the kids in the class were kneeling behind their desks. They looked very serious. The teacher, Ms. Kwan, seemed scary!

Ms. Kwan glared at me. "You're not from the Fire Nation!" she exclaimed.

Oh, no! I'd really been found out this time.

"You are clearly from the colonies," she continued.

"Yeah," I replied, playing along. "I'm from the Fire Nation colonies in the Earth Kingdom. My name is . . . Kuzon."

"You have no manners," Ms. Kwan snapped. "Here in the homeland we bow to our elders."

"Sorry," I said, before bowing to her.

"And we don't cover our heads indoors," she added.

"Uh, I have this scar," I said quickly. "I don't really like anyone to see it."

I was afraid she was going to ask me to take the headband off anyway, but to my surprise, she was okay with it!

Luckily the rest of the day went smoothly. When the school bell rang I headed outside.

A girl started talking to me. "My name is On Ji," she said. "I like your headband."

Then someone called Hidé came up to us. He put his arm around On Ji and stared right at me. "Listen, On Ji is my girlfriend," he said. "Don't forget it!"

Then they walked away.

"It was nice meeting you," I called out.

When I returned to the cave, Katara asked, "Where have you been? We've been worried!"

"I was playing with some kids after school," I said. "And I'm going back tomorrow."

"It's too dangerous to go to a Fire Nation school, Aang!" Sokka exclaimed.

"But I'm learning new things about the Fire Nation," I explained, "like the secret river that leads to the Fire Lord's palace."

Even though they didn't want to, my friends finally agreed that going to school was not a bad idea.

CHAPTER THREE

The next day at school, things didn't go so well. First we had to recite the Fire Nation oath, which I didn't know, so I got into trouble.

Then Ms. Kwan asked, "What year did Fire Lord Sozin battle the Air Nation army?"

I quickly raised my hand. "The Air Nomads didn't have an army," I answered.

The teacher narrowed her eyes. "Do you know more than our history books, Kuzon? Were you there one hundred years ago?"

Actually, I was. But I couldn't tell her that!

Next came music class. But I got into trouble there, too. As I played the tsungi horn I did a little dance with my feet.

"What's wrong with your feet, child?" the music teacher asked.

"I was just dancing," I said. "Don't you dance here in the homeland?"

"No," someone replied. "We don't."

After school, I offered to show On Ji some dance movements.

Suddenly a Firebending blast burned my school book to a crisp. I turned to see Hidé, On Ji's boyfriend, looking angry.

"You're going to show her something?" Hidé snarled.

"Just some dance movements," I said. But this made him even madder.

Hidé struck a combat pose. Then he
charged right at me. I easily stepped away
from the attack.

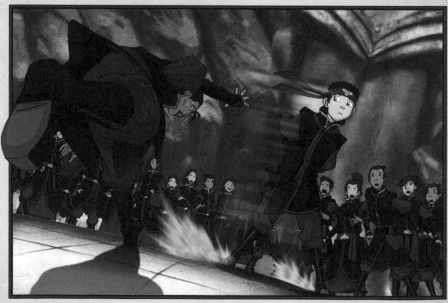

Hidé ended up sprawled on the ground. That's when the headmaster showed up.

"Picking fights on your second day, Kuzon?" he asked.

He thinks *I* started this fight!

"We need to discuss your punishment," he added. "Bring your parents to see me."

"My parents!" I cried. What was I going to do?

CHAPTER FOUR

As usual, Sokka came up with a plan. He put on a fake beard and Katara stuffed a pillow under her dress. They pretended to be my parents.

"Your son has only been here for two days, but he's already causing all kinds of problems," the headmaster explained. "He argued with his history teacher, disrupted music class, and roughed up my star pupil, Hidé."

"My goodness, that doesn't sound like our Kuzon," Katara said.

"If he acts up one more time, I'll have him sent to the coal mines," the headmaster said. "Are we clear?"

"Don't you worry," Sokka said in a deep voice. "This boy is going to get the punishment of a lifetime!"

Later, back in the cave, I came up with an idea. "If we want to change this place for the better, we need to show those kids at school a little taste of freedom."

"What could you possibly do for the little fire monsters?" Sokka asked.

"I'm going to throw them a secret dance party!" I shouted.

CHAPTER FIVE

Everyone helped set up the cave for the party. Toph used Earthbending to create a stage for the band. Katara used Waterbending to set up a fountain for the kids to drink from.

"They're coming!" Toph shouted. "I can feel them approaching the cave. Everyone stop bending."

"You should probably wait outside, buddy," I told Appa. He slipped out the back of the cave.

A bunch of kids from school filed into the cave. Then the school band began playing, but no one was dancing.

"We don't do that here, Kuzon," one of the kids explained.

"Sure you do," I said, remembering how the Fire Nation was a hundred years ago. "I know a few classic Fire Nation dances. Watch!"

Then I showed them a couple of dances.

Next I asked Katara to dance.

"I don't know, Aang," she said nervously.
"I'm not sure how to—"

"Take my hand," I said, reaching out and
leading Katara onto the dance floor. We
spun and whirled and had a wonderful time
dancing.

When we finished, everyone clapped!

After that, everyone started dancing. The kids were even making up their own dance steps. They were all having a great time.

Suddenly the headmaster burst into the cave. A bunch of Fire Nation soldiers were with him—and Hidé too!

You did the right thing by telling me about this party, Hidé," the headmaster said. Then, pointing at me, he shouted to his soldiers, "Get the kid in the headband!"

I turned and dashed into the crowd. The soldiers chased after me.

"Gotcha!" a soldier shouted, grabbing a kid with a headband.

"Looking for me?" the kid asked.

"That's not the one!" the headmaster shouted.

Another soldier grabbed On Ji.

"Yes?" she asked, smiling.

One by one, every kid had put on a headband.

While the school kids kept the soldiers busy, we sneaked out the back of the cave and onto Appa.

"Those kids really helped me by putting on those headbands," I said, as we flew off.

"*You* helped *them*, too, Aang," said Toph. "You taught them to be free."